Sea Fever

'Oh, Saul! What am I going to tell your father?'

'Tell him I don't like it here.'

'*Saul!*'

'Tell him I want to go home.'

Tears spilled over and down her cheeks.

'Saul MacKinnon,' she wailed. 'You thoughtless, insensitive boy! *After what happened to your mother!*'

SHARP SHADES

Sea Fever

Look out for other exciting stories
in the *Sharp Shades* series:

Sea Fever

By Gillian Philip

Published by Evans Brothers Limited
2A Portman Mansions
Chiltern St
London W1U 6NR

British Library Cataloguing in Publication Data
 Philip, Gillian
   Sea fever. - (Sharp shades)
   1. Young adult fiction
   I. Title
   823.9'2[J]

ISBN-13: 9780237537289

Series Editor: David Belbin
Editor: Julia Moffatt
Designer: Rob Walster
Picture research: Bryony Jones

Picture acknowledgements:
istockphoto.com: pp 8, 11, 17, 21, 27, 29, 33, 35,
39, 44, 47 and 50

Contents

Chapter One

Nora screamed. A frantic, ear-splitting shriek. To me it was muffled and watery, but I recognised the sound. Blast. She'd found me.

I stayed underwater, making the

most of it. *Wallowing* in it. The sky above me was the colour of pondwater. Weed streaked it, instead of cloud. The pool was murky but I liked it. I liked the green fronds winding slimily round my limbs. I liked my eyes dilating to find the light.

Now I could make out my stepmother's distorted shape. Sighing out my last bubbles of air, I surfaced to take another breath, and what was coming to me. Cold air shrank the skin on my face. *Dry* air. I winced.

'*Saul MacKinnon! You get out of*

that pond RIGHT now.'

'Coming,' I muttered. 'Keep your wig on.'

'You silly, *stupid boy*. You might have drowned!'

Nora was stumbling down the bank. One hand snatched at me, one at the branch of a ragged birch. Shaking pondwater out of my hair, I stayed out of reach. I was wondering if she'd fall in. Half-hoping…

I saw tears in her eyes, and the guilt kicked in.

'Look at you, you're *soaked*! You're *freezing*!'

'I'm fine,' I said.

Sitting down on the muddy bank,
I grabbed a trainer and wrestled it on
to my bare foot.

She'd stopped trying to snatch me
back from the water's scummy edge.
She didn't dare hug me. She just
stood wringing her hands, reduced
to stupid questions.

'Where are your socks?'

I shrugged.

'Didn't you have *socks* on?'

I studied her, as dirty water trickled
into my eyes and down my neck.

'In a hurry,' I said at last. 'I was in
a hurry.' I glanced longingly at the
dark pond.

'Oh, Saul! What am I going to tell your father?'

'Tell him I don't like it here.'

'*Saul!*'

'Tell him I want to go home.'

Tears spilled over and down her cheeks.

'Saul MacKinnon,' she wailed. 'You thoughtless, insensitive boy! *After what happened to your mother!*'

Chapter Two

What was Nora going to tell Dad?
As if I cared.

Fathers. What they say is *I want
you to be happy. Do what your heart
tells you.*

What they mean is something else again.

After all, he used to say the same to my mother. So three years ago, when I was nine, she left us. She walked dreamily into the sea and let it carry her away. And he was furious with her.

So was I.

Don't swim out past the skerries. I'd known that all my life. *Go past the rocks, and the sea-witch will get you.*

Mum knew that as well as I did. But still she swam past the skerries and out of her depth. We never saw her again. The sea-witch must have

kept her, because her body never
rolled up with the tide, wrapped in
weed. We never found her. They'd
found some poor lost fisherman the
year before, washed up on the
barnacled rocks, one dead hand
drifting in a crab pool.

But not Mum. She just went under
and she never came up.

Dad didn't drown himself, only his
sorrow. Till Nora came along. Nora
pulled him briskly out of his whisky-
swamp before he sank.

But then Nora liked saving people.
It drove me crazy. Her job was in a
call centre, but helping people was

her hobby. She liked to *make* them be happy. She didn't believe in dwelling in the past. She did not like people to get cold or wet.

So Nora also liked double glazing and central heating. I always had to take a deep breath of cool air before I went into the house. Today, the deep breath steadied my nerves as the door closed behind me.

My feet squelched on the fitted carpet. Dad stood up.

I slouched past him, but he called after me, angry.

'Stop that, Saul!'

I turned on my heel. 'Top ot?'

He scowled, and I remembered my nostrils were still shut. I let them snap open. 'Stop what?'

'Holding your breath.'

Oh, it hadn't been for *long*. Only a minute or two. I scuffed the carpet with my sodden trainer. 'The air's dry in here. I hate it.'

'You hate everything. That's your trouble.'

'No. I just hate this place!'

I bolted up to my room and flung both windows wide open. That felt better. A cold wind blew thin rain inside. It dampened curtains, bedclothes, and me.

Dad couldn't have found a home further from water. We had moved as far from the sea as we could be in every direction. Two streets away there was a thin stinking burn, and at first I had to make do with that. It was too small to sink in, but I used to sneak down to it anyway. I'd kneel in the water, and push crisp and fag packets out of the way,

and douse my head.

The pond in the wood was a big improvement. But poor Nora fainted the first time she caught me in it. I got some earful from Dad *that* time.

Seemed I was in for another. When my bedroom door opened I leaned further out, into the dusk and the whipping rain. It was almost like being underwater. Almost.

Dad said, 'You know why we came here?'

'Yeah.' My voice was lost in the wild night.

'I miss your mum.'

'Uh-huh.'

'It scared me, living by the sea,' he said. 'If the same thing happened to you—'

'It didn't happen to her,' I said. 'She did it to herself. She didn't want to be with us any more.' Bitterly I added, 'And you hid her coat.'

'Yes.'

'You stole it. Did that make her stay?'

He looked so miserable I almost felt sorry for him.

'No,' he said. 'But I thought it would.'

Chapter Three

It was long and shapeless, made of
sealskin for warmth. Mum loved
that coat beyond reason.

So it was funny that I'd never seen
her wear it.

I wasn't allowed to touch it. Sometimes she'd put her finger to her lips and smile at me, and pull the coat out of its drawer. She'd unwrap it and sniff it and stroke it longingly. She would press her face against it, and let me do the same. I loved its prickly warmth against my cheek, and its salty smell, but not as much as Mum loved it.

But she never wore it. So I don't know why she was so upset when Dad hid it.

Mum was like me, of course. She loved nothing more than being in the water. Mum was a lot odder than me, though. Eccentric.

Well. To be honest? Mad as a crate of fish.

I didn't mind. I didn't mind that her hair hung loose and wild, and smelt of seaweed. Tiny fronds were always caught in it from her last swim. I didn't mind that she sang to herself in the supermarket. She would lean over the fish counter, breathing in, basking in the chill that came off the ice. Drawing stares. I didn't mind.

Mum used to spin me stories about the seal people. The Selkies, she called them. When I was little I

loved drifting off to sleep, her stories swimming around my head.

But sometimes they didn't send me to sleep. Sometimes they kept me awake. Like when she pretended she was one of them.

One of the Selkies.

When she thought I'd gone to sleep, her voice would turn dreamy and low. If my eyes were shut and I was breathing deeply, she'd go on with her story. Maybe Dad overheard her, listening at my bedroom door. He did that a lot. Maybe he was worried about her. Maybe it was just that he loved her stories too.

So she'd talk, half to me and half to herself. She'd say she missed her home. She'd talk of going back to the seal people one day. And not to worry, but she'd be needing her coat.

That'll be why Dad took it away from her.

And that'll be why she was so upset she drowned herself.

Chapter Four

He was frightened it would happen
again. Well, he'd driven her away
with his fear and his clinging and
his *theft*. And now he was going to
drive me away too.

I dreamed about her that night. I dreamed about her hair with the bits of green weed. My face was buried in it as I cuddled into her. Her skin was cold but warmth seeped through me. She didn't smell like Nora's perfume. She smelt of summer days by the sea: salt and sea-breeze and rockpools. Her skin was wet. It was soaking. Water ran off her.

Now we were underwater. Her hair drifted like weed, longer and longer. It tangled round me, pulled me down and down. Her pale limbs drifted in a current and I drifted after her. Down and down. I wasn't

sad. I could see her drowned body but I wasn't sad. I felt at home.

Something grabbed my hair, yanked me to the surface. It was so sharp it hurt. I had to catch my breath. It wasn't water I was breathing. It was dry air and central heating. I blinked and sat up in bed, gasping. The dream didn't scare me. Waking up did.

I lay awake. My bedside clock told me it was early morning. Headlights swept across the window, and rain lashed the glass. It was good rain but it wasn't enough.

You're never to go near that pond

again, Dad had told me. *It isn't fair
on Nora, and it isn't fair on me.*

Not bothered, you see, about what
was fair on *me*.

35

Well, if he wouldn't take me home,
I'd take myself. I could hitch-hike. I
could jump a train, if this was a
movie. Heck, I could *walk* if I had to.

All I knew was, I couldn't stay
here. It was like a desert to me.

Creeping downstairs, I helped
myself to cans of tuna from the
cupboard, and a can opener. I
fumbled higher, finding dust and
dead spiders. At last I found her
precious coat, wrapped in a
Tesco bag.

When it was all stuffed into my
school backpack I closed the door. I
didn't look back. I walked out into

the night, and scrambled up the wet
path on to the bypass.

I didn't take a waterproof.

Chapter Five

'You're young,' said the lorry driver.

I stared ahead. The windscreen wipers slapped away the rain. Slap-slap. Slap-slap. I licked my lips. The sound and the flying water made me thirsty.

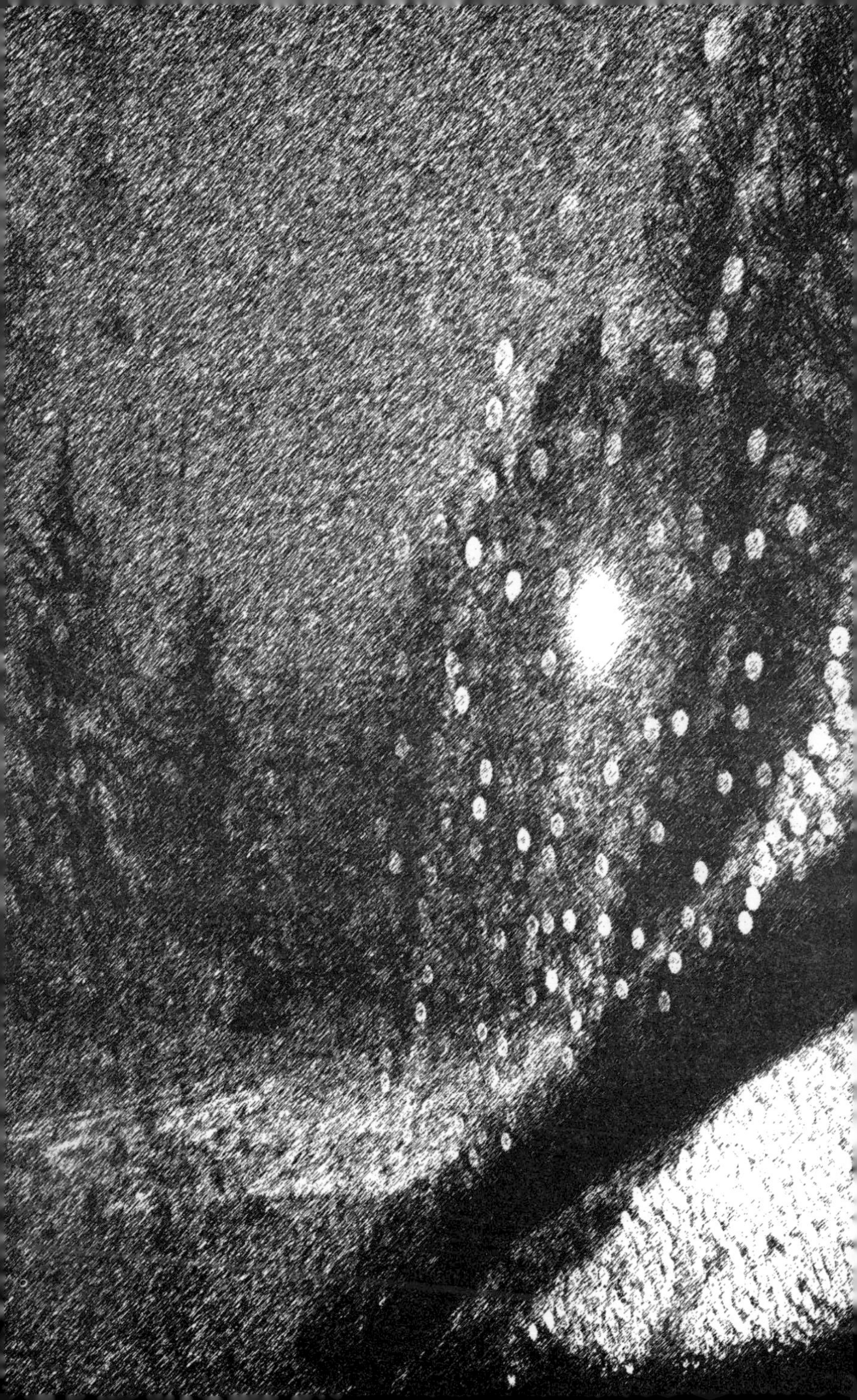

'Bit young to be out on your own.'

'I'm sixteen,' I lied.

'Are you?' He looked doubtful.

I clasped Mum's coat against my chest, wrapped in its bag. My backpack was at my feet. I drummed my heels nervously against it.

'I'm going to see my mum.'

'Does she know you're coming?'

I gave him a withering look. 'Course she does.'

I looked away from him, out of the window. The night was black beyond the motorway. Cold and black. Lovely.

His fingertips drummed the

steering wheel. 'Does she know you're hitch-hiking?'

I shrugged.

Up ahead I saw the glare of a service station. He slewed his lorry on to the slip road and into the car park. It jerked to a halt and the brakes sighed.

'I'll get us something to eat,' he said. 'Won't be long. You coming?'

I shook my head. I didn't want to go in there. Overheated and bright and stifling. I watched the driver slouch towards the sliding doors. His shape was clear against glaring light. That's why I saw him take his

phone from his pocket and thumb
a number.

I fumbled for the door handle and
swung it open.

I jumped to the ground. Turning,
I grabbed my backpack from the
cab. Then I walked casually away
from the lorry. When I was far
enough away, I ran.

Back at the slip road I found a
sign. I knew where I was now. Home
wasn't too far away.

I decided I'd better walk this time.

Chapter Six

A few hours later I was gazing at a
sea like grey silk. The rain had
stopped at last, and a pink sunrise lit
the sand. My feet were sore but I was
happy. The air was bitter, and

deliciously damp.

I could have sat in a rock pool and got myself really wet. That was tempting, but I wanted to delay the thrill. The tide was low and the skerries were exposed, satiny-black. It wouldn't take long to swim out there.

The sea-witch will get you…

My heartbeat sped. Excitement had made me starving, so I hacked open my last can of tuna and ate it with my fingers. Then I pulled out Mum's coat and unfolded it.

The skin felt stiff, and cracked with age. The once-furry pelt was bristly. It still smelt of sea: fish and salt and tangle. Holding it against my face, I inhaled. I was sure it could turn silky and sleek once more.

Out between the skerries and the harbour wall, seal-heads bobbed. There were three of them, black-eyed and solemn. I waved, and one by one they submerged.

Sighing, I stood up and swiped sand off my backside. Best to get on with it.

I waded into the waves. The sealskin coat in my arms was heavy, and my jeans clung to my legs. A wet chill crept up my body. Not fast enough, though. With one hand

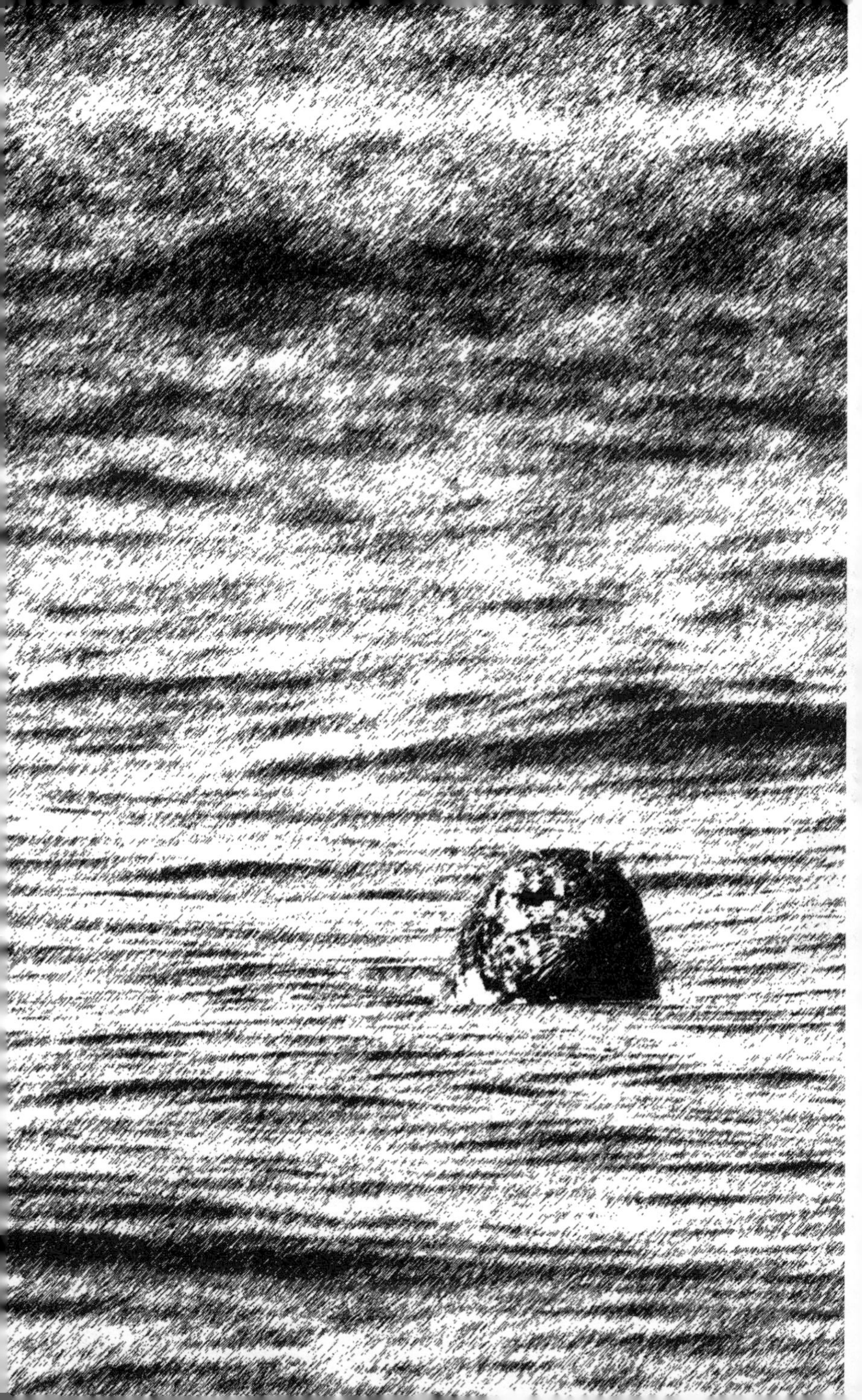

I tugged off my t-shirt and let it float away. That was better. Colder and wetter.

I was up to my chest when I heard a scream.

Dad, I thought. I'd had a good start, but he must have driven all night. He must have broken the speed limit too. I waded faster, trying not to look back.

He must have guessed where I would go. He must have known I'd want to come home.

Well, so he should. I'd told him often enough.

Dad plunged down the sandbank.

He fell, then stumbled up and ran. He was still yelling. He didn't stop at the waves, but they slowed him down. He couldn't move fast in water, not like me. He would never catch up.

'*Saul!*' he howled. 'We'll live here! You can be by the sea!'

I was still in my depth, but only just. I could feel sand sliding between my toes. Kicking up and away, I floated on to my back. The sun was quite high now, and the light dazzled me. I blinked.

'I swear we'll come back!' Dad was still shouting. 'Saul! *Please!*'

Dad was distracting me. It was annoying, so I rolled over and kicked downwards. My head went under the surface. I shut my nostrils as the water closed over my head.

I smiled and closed my eyes. Then I blinked them open, happy. I was in my element.

Tiny silver bubbles were caught in the blond hair on my arms. I could see them in the hairs of the sealskin, too. It was so big and awkward, I thought it would make swimming difficult. It didn't, though. I didn't have to drag it down. It drifted with me. Like it had a life of its own.

My pupils grew wider and blacker as I swam down. I knew that. I could feel them. Weed twined round my ankle, then my wrist.

No, it wasn't weed. It was a slender hand that slipped into mine. Fingers ran through my drifting hair. Lips brushed my forehead, then playfully kissed my nose.

I knew that touch. Not drowned after all.

Well, of course she hadn't. She was my mum.

She hugged me, and her coat. Floating with happiness, I laughed. Bubbles came out.

Tears leaked from her green eyes. Even under water I could see the tears: they looked like little pearls. Pushing back my hair, Mum gave me a pleading look. She squeezed my fingers.

Stay?

I kissed her hand, then hugged her fiercely. Reluctantly I dragged my fingers out of hers.

And then I let go of the coat.

Chapter Seven

As I surfaced, Dad was crying. I
could see him, kneeling in the cold
waves. Jeez. How long was he
planning to wait?

I swam easily towards him. At last

he raised his head. He frowned
and blinked.

His mouth opened. I think he
said, 'Saul?'

I wanted to tell him to get out of
the water. He must be freezing. But I
didn't feel like talking to him yet.

Dad stood up. Shocked, he
floundered towards me, shouting
my name.

I stayed out of reach. Shaking my
wet hair out of my eyes, I trod water.

'You took her coat. *Our coat.*'

'I'm sorry,' he shouted. 'I'm sorry!'

I found my footing in shifting sand.

'Are you?'

'Saul, we'll come back.'

I went on treading water.

'Really?' I asked warily. 'You mean it?'

'I mean it. If that's what you need. I want you to stay with me, Saul. I want you to be happy.'

I smiled. He sounded as if he really meant it. This time he did.

'We'll come back here? You and me and Nora?'

He nodded.

'Yes, Saul. I promise. Honest.'

I could feel someone watching me. Turning in the water, I saw four seal-heads bobbing. They were far out beyond the skerries. I waved.

'So stay with me?' Dad asked, desperately.

I looked back at him. I was still smiling. I couldn't help it.

'Okay.' I swam into his arms. 'I promise too.'

'You do?'

I wrinkled my nose.

'For now anyway.'

'That'll do,' he said.

We were both laughing. And he hugged me so tightly, he nearly drowned us both.

Watch Over Her

'I don't like men who say they're from the Water Company and come inside your flat,' said Anne.

There were no more games. The children didn't seem to like Mrs Cattermole's story. Soon they left and Mrs Cattermole heard their voices softly die away.

Soldier Boy

Soldier Boy

'Did you move them?' asked Martin.

'Why?'

'The finger is curved now.' It was true.

'Yes, I moved them,' Drew said quickly. He shuddered. He wiped the window quickly. He didn't want Martin to realise what he now knew. The finger had written on the window. He had heard it scratching on the glass in the night.

SHARP SHADES

WRONG
EXIT

Mary Chapman

Wrong Exit

'We should be able to see the roundabout,' said Adam.

'There isn't one,' said Dave.

The wide road stretched ahead, absolutely straight, for a mile or more. The roundabout had disappeared, and so had the road that should have led us back to the car.

Where was it? Where was Mum? And where on earth were we?